HE LOST, HE LOST!

Songs, Cartoons, and Commentary
Showing 4 Major Reasons Trump Lost

Sandi Derring

Illustrated by Nick Alexander

HE LOST, HE LOST!

Copyright © 2021 by Sandi Derring

REVIEWS

"He Lost, He Lost! is a fun, yet insightful look into the malignant narcissist that just left the White house. It is an easy read that 80,000,000 of us can enjoy."
> Charles E Hooper
> Speaker Coach.
> Sacramento, California
> www.SpeakerPresenter.com

 "If you need a good laugh during this trying time, check out this new book. It's an SNL literary approach with great illustrations and satire."
> John Covert
> Crystal Image Variety Band
> Jackson, California
> www.crystalimageband.weebly.com

"This book brings some laughs and light in a dark time. Sure to make you smile. For me it's a must read."
> Mark Gagnon
> Film Critic
> Los Angeles, California

TABLE OF CONTENTS

PREFACE

Now that Trump has really lost and is planning to head back to Florida, *He Lost, He Lost!* features some satiric cartoons and commentary illustrating the four main reasons Trump lost. But first it begins with some new songs that explain and celebrate his loss. Each song has a link to the recording on YouTube.

LOSER

WHAT IF A LOSER REFUSES TO LOSE?

https://youtu.be/MyW_QUWNSNA

CHORUS

What if a loser refuses to lose?
When can the winner say it's a win?
What if the loser changes the rules?
When can the winner's win really begin?

VERSE

If a loser in a race should claim that he won,
A photo can show who won by a nose.
So no more disputes, those are final results.
The snap shows the winner, and that's how it goes.

CHORUS

What if a loser refuses to lose?
When can the winner say it's a win?
What if the loser changes the rules?
When can the winner's win really begin?

VERSE

In tennis, a shut-out is love and zero.
There's no way to get back the love that was lost.
The loser can yell and scream all he wants,
But being uncourtly comes at a cost.

BRIDGE

So why do we let politicians
Drag things out and cry fraud or foul.
When it's time to declare "Game is over,"
No more do-overs should be allowed.

VERSE

In sports there are rules about winning.
Accepting a loss is good sportsmanship.
To know when to quit is part of the game.
But the political game is a power trip.

CHORUS

What if a loser refuses to lose?
When can the winner say it's a win?
What if the loser changes the rules?
When can the winner's win really begin?

HE LOST, HE LOST

https://youtu.be/t4aLWWIXvdo

CHORUS   Time to celebrate, he lost, he lost.
He tried to be king, but at such a heavy cost.
The people spoke, they want his reign to end.
We need a caring leader once again.
Not a money and power-loving boss.
It's time to celebrate. He lost!

VERSE   In towns all around
The celebration grows
He tried to hang on,
But now everyone knows.

CHORUS   Time to celebrate, he lost, he lost.
He tried to be king, but at such a heavy cost.
The people spoke, they want his reign to end.
We need a caring leader once again.
Not a money and power-loving boss.
It's time to celebrate. He lost!

VERSE   That's the way it goes
Throughout the land.
Once the king is gone
The power changes hands.

CHORUS   Time to celebrate, he lost, he lost.
He tried to be king, but at such a heavy cost.
The people spoke, they want his reign to end.
We need a caring leader once again.
Not a money and power-loving boss.
It's time to celebrate. He lost!

WHEN A KING GOES MAD

https://youtu.be/AGIIAXQvHgQ

CHORUS

When a king goes mad, it's very sad,
His followers feel lost, they miss what they had.
'Cause his ruling power is gone, and he feels all alone,
While the rest of the world keeps moving on.

VERSE

Though he can complain again and again
Most people can see he's nuts, and then...
Though he tries to rebel with a rebel yell,
 His attempts at a coup won't end very well.

CHORUS

When a king goes mad, it's very sad,
His followers feel lost, they miss what they had.
'Cause his ruling power is gone, and he feels all alone,
While the rest of the world keeps moving on.

VERSE

But when it finally ends, the country will mend,
'Cause now he's lost most of his friends.
Then time to rebuild; he's no longer in.
He's off the stage; a new act can begin.

BRIDGE

Yes, sometimes a peaceful protest,
Can be something the country needs,
But when it's just hatred and violence,
It can never succeed

CHORUS

When a king goes mad, it's very sad,
His followers feel lost, they miss what they had.
'Cause his ruling power is gone, and he feels all alone,
While the rest of the world keeps moving on.

THEY'RE PLAYING POLITICAL GAMES

https://youtu.be/wRp_IufKmKM

CHORUS
They're playing political games.
The only goal is to win
So they may change sides, they might tell some lies,
Based on who's out and who's in.

VERSE
They may offer support to someone
Just to get into their boat.
They look for which way the wind's blowing
'Cause all they want is your vote.

CHORUS
They're playing political games.
The only goal is to win
So they may change sides, they might tell some lies,
Based on who's out and who's in.

VERSE
They play the game for connections,
But they don't have a heart.
They really don't offer solutions.
They just play it safe and smart.

BRIDGE
So what if you have a cause,
A mission to get something done.
Just show it's worth cash, that's all that they ask,
It's a way they can say "I won!"

VERSE
There's a way to get them on your side,
You just have to grease the wheels.
A donation makes it all legal,
The art of the political deal.

CHORUS
They're playing political games.
The only goal is to win,
So they may change sides, they might tell some lies,
Based on who's out and who's in.

ARE WE GONNA HAVE A CIVIL WAR?

https://youtu.be/fc5G7hOQK8w

CHORUS

The rich keep getting richer and the poor keep getting poorer.
Many rich find others' misery easy to ignore
While the poor feel they can't succeed any more.
So are we gonna have a civil war?

VERSE

People are out of work and out of money,
What can they do, where can they go?
They feel so hopeless, life is falling apart,
The fight against injustice is the only path they know.

CHORUS

The rich keep getting richer and the poor keep getting poorer.
Many rich find others' misery easy to ignore
While the poor feel they can't succeed any more.
So are we gonna have a civil war?

VERSE

Many can't pay their mortgage or rent,
So those people out of work are now homeless, too.
There are growing protests in most every state,
And those in power don't know what to do.

BRIDGE

Now the time's running out.
The people need some help.
Till they return to work,
They can't support themselves.
Without money they may feel
They have just one solution.
They have to fight to survive,
And that means revolution.

CHORUS

The rich keep getting richer and the poor keep getting poorer.
Many rich find others' misery easy to ignore
While the poor feel they can't succeed any more.
So are we gonna have a civil war?

INTRODUCTION

HE LOST, HE LOST! features four major reasons that Trump lost - not just the election but popular support, based on a series of cartoons with a spirit of levity. The copy is written in this same spirit, while providing some background to explain the comparisons made in the cartoons.

The four reasons Trump lost are these:

- Trump is Batty, in that Trump can be compared to a bat who is flying blind because he can't see what's real very well. And he running or running away like a bat out of hell.

- Trump Is Nuts, in which Trump is compared to a variety of nuts from peanuts to cashews and pecans, and finally he is carted off to the nuthouse.

- Trump Is an Animal, showing that Trump is like a male animal fighting for power, women, and territory;

- Trump is like a Variety of Extinct Animals or Humans, which compares Trump to dinosaurs and other extinct creatures.

REASON #1: TRUMP IS BATTY

THE BATTY TRUMP BAT

Here are several reasons why Trump is batty like a bat.

Just as bats are the only mammals capable of long and sustained flight, so Trump can easily hop in Air Force One and fly anywhere. And now that he has lost there are fears, he may fly away to seek refuge in another country, most notably Russia, to avoid the prospects of bankruptcy and the many criminal investigations about fraud and other crimes that await, especially in New York. Even his neighbors in Florida don't want him living at Mar-A-Lago, which is designated as a private club, so he may not be able to live there either.

Bats are also considered more maneuverable than birds, because they fly with very long spread-out digits covered with a thin membrane. That's true of Trump, too, because he has used lies to maneuver his way out of almost anything, and he has a very thin skin, so he is easily insulted and angered. Then, he goes after whoever has angered him with insults or plots to seek revenge, and he rouses up his followers to go on the attack, targeting everyone from Hillary Clinton and John McCain to the hosts on Fox News.

Then, too, bats may carry bacteria and viruses which can be harmful to humans, so that people who are not trained and vaccinated should not handle bats. That's true of Trump, too, as he has become a superspreader of the coronavirus himself or has put on superspreader events, such as rallies and White House get-togethers, where thousands of followers and dozens of staffers have gotten sick.

Finally, during the darkest part of the night, common vampire bats, found in the tropics of Mexico, Central America, and South America, emerge to hunt. They feed on people, as well as sleeping cattle and horses, by drinking their victim's blood for about 30 minutes. In fact, they are the only mammals that feed entirely on blood, and they do so when it is very dark, which has given rise to the Dracula stories, originally written about by Bram Stoker in 1897. Well, as they say, Trump sends out many of his Twitter blasts in the dark of night while sitting on the toilet --

and he certainly has blood on his hands, given that over 300,000 individuals have died from the coronavirus, although he claimed it would miraculously go away and an adviser urged him to adopt a strategy of letting people die to gain herd immunity. So for several months, Trump did nothing to stop the virus. Plus there are the deaths of the hundreds of immigrants, including children, who suffered from terrible conditions in the camps, which were like the Nazi concentration camps.

So yes, Trump is definitely batty or has bats in the belfry, as the popular description of people who are crazy goes. Also, a person running quickly can be described as a "bat out of hell," and Trump has a lot of experience with running quickly -- from running for president and maybe now just running away as fast as possible now that he has lost – though there has been talk of him declaring a national emergency to stage a military coup, which is just bats.

REASON #2 - TRUMP IS NUTS!

A key reason Trump lost the election and much popular support is because he has engaged in all kinds of nutty behavior. Thus, the following cartoons compare Trump to a variety of nuts -- from peanuts and cashews to pecans and hazelnuts.

This kind of nutty behavior has increased from the days when Trump was running and then elected President, as claimed by many people, including psychiatrists, psychologists, doctors, academics, and even Trump's niece, Mary Trump, a psychologist and certified life coach. She wrote about her uncle in her book: *Too Much and Never Enough: How My Family Created the World's Most Dangerous Man*, and she has spoken about him in dozens of interviews.

Examples of Trump's nutty behavior abound, including rambling rants at rallies, angry disjointed tweets, delusions about a deep state out to get him, and strange behaviors. These behaviors include getting off a plane and wandering along aimlessly instead of entering his waiting limo, and talking about Frederick Douglass, the famous black abolitionist who died in 1895, getting more recognition, as if Douglas is alive today.

In fact, this comparison with nuts might inspire a whole new brand for Trump -- a line of Trump Nuts, to join Trump Vodka, Trump Steaks, Trump Airlines, Trump University, and other failed ventures. So why not Trump Nuts, featuring all kinds of nuts packed in a gold gift box and shipped right to your door.

The following cartoons illustrate Trump in all his nuttiness.

A WHOLE LOT OF NUTS

Besides being nutty himself, Trump attracted all kinds of nuts who supported him -- from angry White supremacists who were afraid of losing power in an increasingly diverse America to deranged killers who went on shooting rages to commit hate crimes. Trump also played up to the nuts at his rallies where he spewed hate against his latest enemies.

But when you get mixed nuts, you can't be sure of what you are getting, just that they will be mixed up. Likewise, the nuts who became Trump's supporters are a very mixed-up lot, though they aren't very diverse. In fact, a lot of these nuts don't want to be mixed with others at all. They would prefer to be in their own separate jar and hope that others will buy what they are selling.

Mixed Nuts

Is Trump really a nut case? That's what more and more people believe, including some psychologists who have described him as being a "malignant narcissist" or having a "narcissistic personality disorder," whereby one thinks that everything is about "me, Me, ME." Someone with this disorder also has delusions of grandeur about who they are and what they can do. Such a person can never be wrong and is ready to attack anyone who stands in their way, disagrees, or criticizes them. They always have to win whatever they do, and they make excuses should they lose at anything, so they still come out on top. That's a reason why Trump kept refusing to concede the election. So he continued claiming he won after losing over 30 election fraud cases in court, and he kept announcing he had won, even as Biden put together his cabinet and selected officials for Chief of Staff, Secretary of State, and other posts.

Then, too, as Trump sees it, if you're not with him, you're against him and are fair game for insults, threats, and whatever else he can do to demean and humiliate you, whether in the media or in court. As such, he shares traits with other larger-than-life leaders like Hitler and Mussolini, to whom he is often compared, and some consider them nutcases, too. Trump also admires dictators like Vladimir Putin and Kim Jong Un and aspires to become a dictator or king himself. Some examples include: having a military parade in front of the White House; calling on the police to clear away protesters so he could pose for a photo with a Bible in front of St. John's Church in Lafayette Square; and conducting Hitler style rallies from the White House balcony and around the country. Plus he has readily fired almost anyone who dared to disagree with him, often announced with a tweet.

It's a Nut Case

POWER NUTS

Another reason Trump lost is because he's is like the cashew nut. Just call him the Trumpking Nut, because he aspired to be a dictator or king, to whom the laws didn't matter. Thus, he felt he could do whatever he wanted, since he was above the law as the most powerful ruler in the world. That's why he hired staff members and placed others in different government departments and agencies, so they would be ready to do his bidding. And they did, since he was in power and they were afraid of standing up to him and being fired.

Trump might also be like the cashew nut, because, as they say, "cash is king", and if you've got the cash or cachet, anyone can be king or at least act like one. But if you lose your cash or cachet, you're out of luck, because without the royal accoutrements, like a fancy robe, scepter, and crown, one can be just like other mixed up nuts in the world. And such nuts can easily get stepped on and squashed.

Yet, for four years, Trump did many nutty things, as he aspired to be a king or emperor. To this end, he regularly flouted laws, got the government to pay money to further his business interests, such as his hotels and golf courses. For example, when he went on trips and the government had to foot the bill for his travel and the cost of rooms and meals at his properties. Then, too, he ran the White House like the court of a king, where those who worked there were like courtiers and servants. That's also why Trump sought out the flattery of strong rulers like Putin and Xi Jinping, and ordered people around like a mob boss. And like such rulers and bosses, he sought lots of cash and spent lavishly on his travel, golf, and building projects for his business. Plus he gave tax breaks to the rich and powerful, even while more and more people were losing homes, jobs, and businesses in the pandemic. Now isn't that nuts? But finally, Trump lost his cachet and was voted out.

The Trumpking Nut

In some ways, Trump is like the macadamia nut, which is a round, hard shelled nut that came to the U.S. from Australia by way of Hawaii. So it might be considered like a tough military nut called the Trump Military Nut, known for its strength and prowess as a tough nut to crack -- a quality Trump likes to have.

Yet, because it comes originally from Australia, the macadamia nut is not really American. So it's like an immigrant nut, which like most other immigrants, according to Trump, should be deported and never allowed to return. After all, from the beginning of his presidency, Trump tried to deport undocumented immigrants from the U.S. and keep other immigrants from coming in from Mexico. In the process, he had ICE officials put thousands of immigrant parents and kids in cages, and they separated over 500 kids from their parents. At the same time, in true military spirit, Trump has launched trade wars with China and alienated allies in Canada and Europe.

Trump Military Nut

Another apt comparison is with the sunflower seed, which is a tough seed which can grow anywhere and spread its flowers all over the land, just like Trump has been spreading Trumpism everywhere to his army of followers. So as the Trumpflower Seed, Trump is like a warrior gathering his armies to attack and take down anything in his path -- even the American Eagle and all it represents – from the democratic courts to the laws of the land.

The Trumpflower just has to spread enough of its seeds throughout the countryside, and soon there will be Trumpflowers everywhere. Then, as the Trumpflower grows up big and strong, any plants in its way will soon wither and die, as will many birds and other animals.

But will the Trumpflower prevail in spreading its seeds? Stopping the spread is why so many millions of people rose up to stop Trump's efforts to overturn many environmental protections, so he could let the oil and gas companies drill and drill or frack and frack. And that's why millions have risen up to protest the many things he has done to spread hate and despair, such as by breaking up of families by deporting immigrants and ignoring the threat of COVID-19 while millions suffered and died. Trump even put on dozens of superspreader rallies and other events that led the virus to spread even more -- a little like Nero fiddling while Rome burned.

The Trumpflower Seed

Trump is like the hickory nut, too, in that it is a very hard nut to crack. It is known for its hard, nearly unbreakable shell, and the hickory tree's shaggy bark was considered perfect for making hickory sticks and switches, used to strike fear into anyone in danger of being hit. No wonder, at times, hickory became the rod of choice by jailers and schoolteachers for punishing anyone, when such punishments were legal.

Likewise, during his presidency, Trump was often a great advocate for using this stick along with other methods of torture, including waterboarding, to bring any miscreants, to what he considered justice. Then, too, Trump is like a hickory nut in the way he has sought to crack down on anyone he suspects has been disloyal to him - by insulting them, firing them, suing them, and otherwise creating all sorts of obstacles in their life. So call it the Trump Hickory Nut Special, and consider it one more Trump brand.

The Trump Hickory Nut Special

TOUGH NUTS

Trump is like a walnut, which might be called a Wall Nut, since it has a very strong, hard exterior that's great for creating walls, as well as building all kinds of furniture. At the same time, the walnut's exterior covers up a soft interior, much like a person might be strong on the outside to protect their inner insecurity, which is what many psychologist claim about Trump. Outside he has acted very macho and has been ready to call others "losers," but inside he is very afraid of being weak or being considered a "loser" himself.

Another way that Trump might be compared to a walnut is that its inner nut is composed of two sections, which look much like the lobes of a human brain, where the left side is linked to being rational, and the right side to being intuitive and emotional. If the two sides of the brain are in balance, great. Otherwise, one's emotions can erupt out of control, which is why Trump has sometimes been portrayed like a baby or toddler having a tantrum -- or maybe call it a tantrump -- when he becomes angry about something and erupts in a rage.

Plus the walnut' s exterior can be like the wall of a castle – keeping anyone and everyone out. And more than anything, Trump wants a wall between Mexico and the U.S. But while only a few miles got built and many walls blew over after they were built, Trump managed to build a high wall around the White House as protection from the angry protestors outside.

The Trump Wall-Nut

Trump is also much like the pecan, a nut with old Southern roots, so it's no wonder the Trump Pecan Delight is proud of its old Southern traditions -- from delicious pecan pies to KKK hoods, which are shaped like the end of a pecan. Just poke in two holes and paint the pecan nut white, and voila, it looks like a hood. Then, too, since the pecan has a smooth, thin shell, it's perfect for heating up to make a pecan pie. But don't stir it up too much, because due to its thin skin, it could easily explode and make a big mess – in the kitchen or elsewhere, just like the KKK and other White supremacist groups are making a big mess of things today in the U.S.

Also, in keeping with the pecan's Southern roots, Trump has many conservative Deep South supporters, including some good old boys from the KKK and Proud Boys. He even told the Proud Boys to "stand up and stand by," presumably to be ready to fight any protestors and dissuade voters during the election. And now since Trump lost, they might still be standing by to cause trouble to show their continued support for Trump and undermine Biden's efforts to bring the divided U.S. back together.

The Trump Pecan Delight

Just like the Pumpkin Seed, the Trumpkin Seed is one tough cookie...er seed, since it's not really a nut. Rather, it's a very strong seed, which comes from the pumpkin, a large, pulpy round fruit with a thick, orange-yellow rind that looks very much like Trump, who is sometimes called the Orange Man. With a few deep knife cuts, you can carve out the eyes, nose, and mouth to make a perfect Trump-O-Lantern, which has been often shown on the social media to mock Trump as a scary monster or clownish joke.

Then, too, Trump might be thought of like a Trumpkin Seed, who just wants to win. Or perhaps consider him more like a bad seed from the Trumpkin Patch, where winning at any cost is the name of the game; otherwise you're a loser and sucker, as Trump once called the U.S. soldiers who died in the wars. Likewise, Trump sought to take on the coronavirus by thinking it would go away like a miracle. So he tried to ignore it, he persuaded his followers to ignore science and the virus in order to keep the economy going to assure his reelection. But the opposite happened, as more and more people died, many his own followers, and he came down with the virus himself. So did several dozen White House staffers, Secret Service agents, and many others who attended his superspreader events, such as the confirmation ceremony for Amy Coney Barrett, the judge he nominated to the Supreme Court.

The Trumpkin Seed Wins Again

MONEY NUTS

Trump, as the Hazeltrump Nut, shares some qualities with the hazelnut, which comes from a variety of small shrubs or trees in North America and Europe and has a smooth brown shell. It is most known for its creamy spread, so it has been packaged as a great spread that you can put over anything. Thus, it can easily be spread everywhere and anywhere, much like Trump has become a superspreader of everything -- from misinformation and economic ruin for millions to the coronavirus.

But while the hazelnut can make an ideal surface spread, if you clump a lot of it together, it can turn into a pile of...well, something you want to get rid of, which is what over 80 million people did in the election by voting for a change to a more soothing and unifying Biden presidency.

Hazeltrump Nut

Trump is also like a wingnut, which has a pair of projections which go around in circles to tighten a screw. Likewise, the Trump Wingnut can go in circles, as he changes his mind back and forth and sometimes forgets or claims he didn't say or agree to something he did, such as when he first was against a stimulus, then for one, and finally didn't act to provide one for those who were unemployed or in failing businesses due to the pandemic.

A wingnut has also become an American political term that refers to a person who holds extreme, and often irrational, political views, primarily right wing, and that certainly characterizes Trump to a wingnut.

Then, too, the Trump Wingnut is like a trendy brand name that Trump has used to brand everything with the Trump name, such as steaks, vodka, casinos, hotels, buildings, health products, and a university, though many brands failed, contributing to Trump's six bankruptcies between 1991 and 2009. And now under the Trump presidency, the U.S. economy is on the verge of a great recession, too, due to unemployment, business failures, and the pandemic.

Thus, like a wingnut, Trump is the expert in screwing around, screwing up, and screwing anyone considered disloyal, which is one reason so many people voted with about 80 million votes for Joe Biden -- to stop Trump from screwing up the country even more.

The Trump Wingnut

NUTTIEST NUTS

Trump is also like the coconut, since it's got a hard shell outside, with lots of fuzzy barbs. So it looks like a head covered with frizzy hair, much like Trump's hairpiece, once blonde, but now coconut white. Likewise, the Trump Coconut or Trumponut is all white inside, just like White supremacists think things should be.

Unfortunately, though, when coconuts fall from the trees in the tropics, they can crack open. That's how many coconuts get cracked up, and then an army of ants can eat them up, much like an army of protesters appeared at many of Trump rallies and events -- and then began celebrating in the streets at Trump's fall from his White House platform.

The Trumponut

Trump also shares key characteristics with the pistachio nut, which comes from the Mediterranean region and Western Asia, but mostly is known for having an oily green kernel under its small hard shell. That's why pistachio ice cream is green, too.

While Trump doesn't like the greens associated with the environment or climate change, such as the Green Deal, featuring practices to protect the environment, he likes many others greens -- especially the greens on golf courses, the lush green of elegant lawns, and having plenty of greenbacks for spending money.

Thus, being the Trump Pistachio Nut fits him to a T for Trump – and it makes a great tea, which could be packaged and sold as one more Trump brand to buy.

But one other green has contributed to Trump's undoing -- being very green or new at something, which increases the chance of failure. So it's no wonder he has failed at so many things he is new at, such running the government after never holding a political office but gaining fame as a reality TV star on *The Apprentice.* Thus, it has been a rough term in office, marked by years of chaos, confusion, firings, scandals, and lawsuits. Then, too, being so green, he doesn't know what he doesn't know. Or he doesn't want to know or doesn't care, such as not wanting to read intelligence briefings and preferring to play golf on his greens. And many of the White House staffers, agency appointees, and members of his legal team have been green at what they are doing, too, which has contributed to the chaos, confusion, and finally losing the election, so no second term.

Pistachio Trumpnut

Trump's parallels with the nutmeg offers still other reasons why Trump lost. For example, people who act crazy are sometimes called "nutty as a fruitcake." But they might also be called nutty as a "nutmeg," because the it not only adds a spicy flavor in cooking, but in higher doses, it is an aphrodisiac and has psychoactive effects, making people go super nuts.

As a result, they might have all kinds of delusions, such as thinking that they are more powerful than they are or that there is a deep state conspiracy out to get them, so they have to take steps to defeat it. Then, if they are persuasive enough, they can get many thousands or millions to believe in the conspiracies -- or they can believe the conspiracy theories of others and persuade their followers to accept those conspiracies as real, too.

That's just what Trump has done in sharing his delusions at rallies or in tweets with the persuasive skills of a super salesperson getting others to believe. And so he has gotten his followers to follow him and do what he wants, even as his rallies and tweets have gotten crazier and crazier in the last weeks of his campaign and Presidency. Plus he has been spreading COVID-19 to the crowd of mostly unmasked followers who go nuts with their wild cheers for him and their put downs for those they disagree with, such as by chanting "Lock him up!" or "Lock her up!" And some have done even crazier things because of their fervent belief, such as crashing their cars into protestors or shooting people on the street or in malls.

The Nutty Nutmeg

NO MORE NUTS

Sometimes things can go wrong, when you don't know what you are doing or you end up with a screw loose. Then, people can turn on you, so you get really screwed and screwed up, such as when Trump's former lawyer Michael Cohen and many former staffers, agency heads, and military officials decided enough was enough and spoke out against him. Plus many White House staffers secretly leaked stories to the media describing the chaos and confusion in the White House, which Trump promptly labeled fake news and looked for the leaker.

In turn, all of that leaking, backbiting, and internal and external fighting helped to contribute to Trump's loss. It's like when you get a package of nuts in their shells. Usually, people throw away the shells and enjoy the nut, but in this case, a growing number of people just wanted to throw away the nut. So Trump was screwed by being voted out. And many who voted that way did so thinking him a screwed up screw-up.

Screwed Up and Screwed

Trump is also like that acorn that falls from a tree and then gets stepped on or squashed by a squirrel.

While big oaks might grow from little acorns, that's only some of the time for this thick-walled nut that's usually set in a woody, cuplike base. Unfortunately, some oaks can get off to a very bad start, such as if they are stepped on by a passing hiker or eaten by a squirrel. Then, too, as the climate gets warmer and warmer, a budding oak tree can shrivel up and die, because it is too hot and dry. It could even be consumed by a fire from lightning or blown up in a war. And sometimes small white worms can worm their way into these acorns. So instead of the acorn being the beginnings of a strong, sturdy oak, out pops a small wiggly worm.

Likewise, the Trump Accorn has finally met its match, as protesters and voters have finally pushed him down and out.

Trump Acorn

Finally, a reason Trump lost is that the White House, for many, became a kind of nuthouse, led by the Nut in Chief. There was so much chaos and confusion, as Trump kept changing his mind, striking out against a former ally or friend, throwing out insults like pitch balls at a game, and discarding many people around him like pawns in a chess game. So maybe the system became nuts, because of all the nuts who were running the nuthouse, as in *One Flew over the Cuckoos' Nest* or *King of Hearts*.

And what is especially nuts is the way Trump, his senior officials, and other staffers acted like COVID-19 wasn't a threat. Then, several dozen of those in the White House got it, including Trump. No wonder the White House got turned into a nuthouse, and after Trump leaves, he could end up in a regular nut house, too.

Welcome to the Nuthouse

REASON #3: TRUMP IS LIKE A MALE ANIMAL SEEKING POWER, TERRITORY, AND FEMALE CONQUESTS

The following cartoons show Trump as one of the many male animals who struggle with other males for power, territory, and females. The struggles are all about showing dominance, so the top dog or alpha male in the group can show the other males and females who is boss. He gets the best perks while in charge -- such as the most grooming and the best locations. Plus, eager females are ready, willing, and able to mate with him, though as he gets older, he mainly seeks to control them. At the same time, the dominant male always has to be alert to defend himself from other males vying for the top spot, as they repeatedly seek to dethrone him. When one does, he becomes the new king of the herd, pack, or tribe.

MAMMALS

Just as kangaroos from Australia have long been known for their fighting prowess, as they raise their paws much like a human boxer and have large sharp claws on their hands and feet to do extensive damage in a fight, so Trump has used everything he's got to go after his adversaries. Also, just as kangaroos have a thick stomach skin that protects them from serious injury, so they can soon fight again, so Trump has bounced from a fight with one group to another. It doesn't matter if the adversary is in the U.S. or abroad, he is ready to fight, and no matter how much any individual, group, or government official goes after him with insults or report on his latest gaffes, he keeps coming back to fight some more. But now more and more, he is increasingly losing the ability to fight a winning fight.

Kicking Kangaroos

Just as Coyotes are known for being wily and tricky, and commonly win by intimidation, Trump has resorted to tricks and lies, such as making up fibs about competitors and frequently changing his policies. Then, too, like a coyote quickly changing directions to lead pursuers astray, Trump is a master of attacking opponents with a mix of angry words, barks, growls, and other sounds. If things don't go his way, he is continually howling and whining about something being unfair or the system being rigged, though he considers it fine if he is unfair to others.

Cunning Coyotes

Chimpanzees have always been fighters – just like Trump. It's like an ape fight ape world, in which the winners are rewarded with food and mates. It's a world in which bands of chimps violently kill individuals from neighboring groups to expand their territory, much like Trump seeks to overcome rivals to acquire new properties all over the world.

Chimps also use all kinds of tools to fight with – from tree branches and sticks to clubs they find on the ground, whatever it takes to beat down an opponent and show who's boss. Though Trump uses documents, smart phones, and lawyers, the principle is the same – do whatever you must to win and keep winning!

Also, like chimps, Trump fights for everything – which has gotten him some great prizes, such as beautiful women as wives, mistresses, and lovers, and real estate properties all over the world. However, just as happens with chimps, not all of Trump's fights are successful, so he has lost some properties, gained massive debts, and now lost the Presidency. So, much as chimp leaders have to retire in disgrace after losing a dominance struggle to another male, so has Trump been forced to concede the fight, despite fighting with battalions of lawyers, who are like the subordinate chimps joining the battle to support their leader.

Chimp Champion

Trump is also like a baboon in many ways. Baboons, characterized by long dog-like muzzles, powerful jaws, sharp canine teeth, and thick fur, are known for being very baaad -- especially the dominant males, who can be very nasty. They intimidate other in the troop and lurking predators, and they bite with their large canines, leaving death and destruction in their wake. Additionally, they act like kings of the savannah, woodland, and hills across Africa, as they eat almost everything, and they are known for their loud vocal exchanges which help to demonstrate their dominance.

Likewise, Trump, well-known for his furry hairpiece, likes to dominate and intimidate anyone he can, whether in his Republican Party troop or in the Democratic Party. He is ready to attack other countries, too, especially Mexico, China, and the countries in Central or South America, because he wants to keep out their. To do so, he claims he'll do whatever it takes, from waterboarding and killing the families of terrorists to separating family members at the border and getting better deals. Should you dare to oppose him, he's ready to attack, whether through nasty tweets, complaints to the media, or lawsuits for millions of dollars, which are like the loud vocal exchanges of the baboons. He is like the baboons taking on all comers on the savannah or woodlands, using any methods they can to get their way.

Baaad Ass Baboons

Like the African elephant, the largest living terrestrial animal, Trump emphasizes bigness in everything, and likes everything to be BIG and GREAT! No wonder he spent lavishly in redecorating the White House and building walls around it. Plus he spent big government bucks on travel, golf club excursions, and stays at his properties around the world.

He also has been GREAT at giving everyone a good show, turning usually boring politics into continually entertaining and humorous events for the past few year. And like bull elephants trying to intimidate or fight their rivals, he got many losers to run away or submit to his power, from staffers to Republican leaders. But then he was defeated by a very small invisible rival -- the great pandemic, along with a very large number of mailed in ballots, and he didn't know how to successfully fight that.

Trumpophants

Hippos are huuuge, as well as highly aggressive and unpredictable, much like Trump, who responds largely from his intuition and whim, and is ever ready to attack anyone for anything deemed insulting or offensive to him. He also likes everything to be "huuge," "great," or otherwise "extraordinary."

Besides being huuge, hippos are especially known for their huge jaws, and apart from eating, the males spend much of their times fighting with other males. Often they fight with their big mouths wide open, a little like Trump's attacks with his big mouth, which he uses to insult and humiliate revivals and defend against any attacks with an even bigger attack to fight back. And Trump knows how to get off a good insult, such as calling someone an "animal...loser...failure...traitor ...spy" or calling any reporting unfavorable to him as "fake news."

The Trumappotamus

Though rhinos are characterized by their large size and thick protective skin, they have relatively small brains for their size, so they are not very bright. And neither is Trump, because he doesn't know much about things that most politicians know about, such as the Constitution or names of some countries. But like a rhino, he can push away the questions that probing journalists ask about his lack of knowledge or misstatements, because of his outer thick skin.

Even so, he doesn't take criticism very well and often responds by going ballistic with a flurry of tweets, because underneath that outer armor, he seems to have a very thin skin. Thus, much like a rhino, he is ever ready to fight, starting with intimidation, and if that doesn't work, a nasty verbal shoving and butting match follows, which can end with the loser gored and defeated through losses to his or her reputation and money. This is why Trump has engaged in so many gory fight-to-the-finish battles with Democrats, other Republicans, his own staffers, the media, and just about anyone else who dared to disagree with him about anything.

Raging Rhinos

Trump is much like the cape buffalo, a short, massive beast, who is one of the most dangerous animal in Africa, as he fights and kills in the water. Likewise, Trump likes to throw his weight around, whether he is negotiating land deals, taking over the Republican Party, or changing the political universe forever. With his bullying tactics, he has buffaloed his way around wherever he is to get what he wants -- including trying to stay in office by falsely claiming massive voter fraud to overturn the election.

Just like the cape buffalo has never been domesticated because its unpredictable nature makes it dangerous to be around, Trump is much the same. He is known for his emotional changing moods, where he quickly shoots from the hip and changes policies and positions almost on a whim, based on what he wants.

Unfortunately, one of the cape buffalo's major weaknesses is being subject to foot-and-mouth disease, an infectious and sometimes fatal viral disease. Similarly, Trump often puts his foot in his mouth on many occasions, and his unpredictable behavior has contributed to his defeat.

The Trumalo

Like the large bighorn sheep of the Rockies, known for their big horns and heavy weight of up to 300 pounds, Trump has made a practice at throwing his weight around. The sheep also have extra thick skulls and neck vertebrae, so they can better absorb the impact of clashes with others and quickly recover to fight again. Much in the same way, Trump seems to go from fight to fight, becoming more and more ferocious and angry at any defeat. Then, too, much like these sheep live in high places, such as alpine meadows, mountain slopes, and the foothills near rugged cliffs, Trump has lived on high in the towers of Manhattan. And like a sheep climbs high to seek cover from many predators, Trump has sought the cover of high-priced lawyers to fight thousands of lawsuits.

The sheep's heavy weight and agility also helps in fights to establish a dominance hierarchy, and they fight like boxers by jumping and lunging at each other with head butts and clashing horns, until the most powerful fighter wins. Similarly, Trump butts heads with many different people, as he seeks to always win and climb to higher and higher heights, while claiming victory even in the face of defeat. But now he has been butted off his White House perch and may never rise again, despite repeated fights to stay on top.

Unfortunately, a potential hazard of living in steep, rugged terrain is getting hit by a rock or falling off a cliff, much like Trump has faced bankruptcy six times. In the past, he had the agility to get back on his feet and climb to the heights again, but now maybe not. Only time and a few more fights will tell.

The Trumphorn Sheep

Like Trump, fur seals like to show they are heavy weights, and they enjoy hanging out in colonies on the beaches, where dominant males mate with more than one female – much like Trump has had three wives, numerous mistresses, and short- term relationships with many beautiful women.

The fur seal males also engage in big fights, until the dominant male maintains his place. But if the usurper wins, the once dominant male loses everything and often slinks off to sea, since he has lost his place in the community. It's a fight that resembles what happened in the political arena, as Trump fought off the Republican Party challengers to become the nominee, fought to become President, and has fought to stay President, despite losing the election. So he refused to leave the White House and kept fighting through his lawyers to overturn the votes in key states. But if he doesn't win, maybe he'll have to slink off like the male fur seal, though instead of disappearing into sea after losing the fight for dominance, he might go off and play golf and do more business deals, since he is out of the political game. But he still has other games to play, more battles to try to win.

Trump Fur Seal

Trump likewise has many traits of the meerkats, who are especially feisty and aggressive, despite being only 12 inches tall. They live all over the Kalahari Desert, where a group of them are called a mob, gang, or clan, much like some Las Vegas casino owners, and at one time, Trump owned the Trump Casino before it went bust.

Meerkats are especially known for the way its family group, typically about 20 individuals, organizes to look for food and avoid predators. A sentry stands guard, watching for predators, such as eagles and jackals, while other meerkats look for food. Having these guards is like the way Trump has bodyguards to watch over him wherever he goes, from his properties to play golf to his rallies seeking support from fans. Should some protesters appear, the bodyguards jump into action, much like the sentry meerkat cries out to warn the others of danger. Then, the foraging meerkats rush home to the safety of their burrow, much like the way Trump's bodyguards lead him to a car and drive away from a protest demonstration. At times Trump has hidden in his bunker, much like meerkats often retreat to their burrow when danger threatens.

Just like the meerkat males are ready to fight to establish dominance over other males and resistant females, so Trump seems ready to take on anyone who stands up to him. One way is calling anyone opposing him a loser, sucker or a derisive nickname. Or Trump fires anyone under his tight family group, Trump has brought family members into his administration as advisers or as surrogates to run his businesses, so he and his family members can profit from the Presidency, and he can better be sure of everyone's loyalty to maintain his power.

The Mighty Trumpkat

BIRDS

Trump might also be compared to the rooster who struts around like he's the cock of the walk, since he has gotten many institutions to do his bidding from Congress to the Justice Department, CIA, and CDC. Just ruffle his feathers and another official is gone, like a downed cock who got cocked.

While roosters normally fight other roosters for dominance, power, and mating rights, and the losers live to fight another day, in cockfighting, two roosters bred for aggression fight to the death, while fans cheer for their bird to win. And that's much like what Trump has done with almost all other Republicans by getting them to follow his lead -- and if they don't, he has aimed to completely destroy the careers, much like a winning rooster seeks to destroy the loser.

Likewise, Trump has been ready to crow about any other battles he has won, even if he has lost along the way, such as in his 4000 lawsuits, six bankruptcies, two divorces, and over a dozen rape claims against him. It's like everything in his life has turned into a fight, while the American public following the saga on the news and social media, might be compared to the spectators watching cocks battle it out in a ring. At the same time, his rapid supporters cheering him on, like the Proud Boys and Boogaloos, might be compared to the fans rooting for their cock to destroy the other bird in a cock fight to the death.

The Trump Cock of the Walk

An image of Trump being attacked by an American eagle seems a fitting image for Trump's relationship with America today. As large, powerful birds of prey, eagles go after what they want and get it. Like all birds of prey, eagles have a large hooked beak to readily rip flesh from their prey, and they have strong muscular legs, powerful talons, and keen eyesight. So once they have their eyes on a likely target, they go after that prey with determination.

This seems like a fitting parallel to what is happening today, since the bald eagle is America's national bird in today's divided America. And Trump has been stoking the division even more, such as with his call out to the Proud Boys who support white nationalism to "stand up and stand by."

Who's gonna win the eagle's attack -- the eagle or Trump? It's like a battle to the finish, and now it seems like the eagle has gained a victory with the winning Biden-Harris ticket. So soon it can soar high again and prevail in these dangerous and divisive times marked by all kind of battles, from wars to the worldwide pandemic.

Eagle Power

REPTILES

Trump can also be compared to the Komodo dragon, the largest living species of lizard found on a half-dozen Indonesian islands, where it can grow up to 10 feet and weigh up to 150 pounds. It is believed to have survived hard times during the Pleistocene because of its large size, so now they essentially rule the roost and successfully hunt and ambush all kinds of prey.

Likewise, at 74, Trump might be viewed as something of a relic who is continually fighting to show he is still strong and powerful. In doing so, he uses various supports to show his power, such as bodyguards to provide a wall of protection when he speaks at a rally. Plus he has a team of lawyers ready to file lawsuits should someone defame or besmirch his name or his properties.

Komodo dragons are similarly great fighters, and one of their weapons is their venomous bite, which might be compared to the venom that Trump often spits out to attack anyone crosses him. And just like the winner of a battle pins the loser to the ground, Trump is ready to attack and hold down anyone who resists his effort to get what he wants.

The Trump Dragon

Trump might be compared, as well, to the anaconda, the largest snake from tropical South America. The anaconda eats other snakes and anything else it can ambush, by squeezing until its victim is asphyxiated. Then, it swallows its prey whole and digests it over the next weeks or months. In like fashion, Trump, who is often called a snake by his detractors, can easily squeeze the life from his competitors, political rivals, and underpaid workers at his hotels and golf courses. Whatever the reason, as Trump puts his squeeze on others by not paying, paying less than due, saying damaging words, or filing suit, the victim commonly succumbs. But just as hunters can kill anacondas or collectors for zoos can bag them, so political and legal opponents have come after Trump to put him out of power, so he can't successfully attack and harm other.

The Trumaconda

Trump is like the Galapagos tortoise, which lives on the Galapagos Islands near Ecuador and Aldabra near Tanzania. They are known for being very huuuge as the largest living species of tortoise, which can grow up to six feet and weigh up to 900 pounds. They also have a very hard shell and short neck, much like Trump claims to have a thick skin. But while he might retreat to his Trump Tower in Manhattan or behind the White House walls, he seems to have a thin skin underneath his outer shell of wealth, property, and political power. That's why he responds with rage like an angry tortoise ready to attack, when anyone says anything he considers a put down, like saying he has less money than he claims to have.

Male tortoises also engage in aggressive behavior with each other, and their fights can include biting and last for many hours before one leaves in defeat. Likewise, once Trump is determined to fight a rival or support a position, the fight can go on for a long time, such as in his last stand to avoid accepting his defeat to Joe Biden.

Finally, Trump is like a tortoise in that tortoises are very slow moving. Likewise, some describe Trump as being lazy, since he shows little interest in learning about government policies and practices. Rather, he likes to say whatever he thinks at the moment, and doesn't want to take time to learn the details, such as in intelligence briefings. As a result, he often gets his information wrong or wants to change his mind after making a choice, such as in deciding whether to pass a stimulus package or not during the pandemic.

The Trump Tortoise

REASON #4: TRUMP IS LIKE A VARIETY OF EXTINCT ANIMALS AND HUMANS

The following cartoons show Trump compared to variety of extinct beasts, such as different types of dinosaurs, extinct birds, and ancient mammals. Plus he shares traits with early humans, such as the Neanderthal.

Why did these creatures go extinct? Maybe, some scientists believe, a big comet crashed to earth and exploded like a nuclear bomb, which killed off the dinosaurs and other species. Or maybe the climate and environment changed causing some species to die out, or maybe more powerful animals wiped out weaker ones, much as might be occurring today.

So this is now, and that was then. But maybe in his battles with politicians, governments, lawyers, and justice officials, Trump could end up like these ancient beasts that went extinct.

DINOSAURS

The Tyrannosaurus Trump is in many ways like the 40 foot 8 ton Tyrannosaurus Rex, who roamed the flood plains, swamps, and forests of Montana and Alberta in the late Cretaceous. Like the Tyrannosaurus, he eagerly gobbles up anything he can overpower, and he enjoys seeing his prey cower in terror or run in fear. Then, when he captures and swallows them, he feels even more power and is ready to conquer, kill, and go after his next target, whether it's the Democrats, Fox News, or the head of one of the government agencies who dared to contradict him with the facts. But now it seems the facts are coming out, and he may have all kinds of legal problems. So no wonder he might be going extinct.

The Tyrannosaurus Trump

The Trumporaptor, is in many ways like the 8 foot 150 pound Velociraptor, who roamed Mongolia and Eastern Asia during the Upper Cretaceous. The Velociraraptor is known for slicing and dicing his prey with his long claw on each hind foot that cuts like a knife. The Trumporaptor similarly attacks, using his words like a knife to cut down those on his enemy list with angry insults. At first he may draw followers to him with his rallies, which are like a religious revival that gets everyone exciting and eager to believe. But should anyone dare to dispute anything he says, such as by mentioning an uncomfortable truth, that's all the Trumporaptor needs to cut and flay his new enemy like a filet of fish. Then, zap! The latest victim is cut down with a barrage of tweets and threats at rallies, so his followers can go after them too. Then, the Trumporaptor is on to the next victim to satisfy his rapacious hunger for more and more enemies to undergo more slicing and dicing.

The Trumporaptor

The Brontotrumpus is in many ways like the 80 foot 30 ton Brontosaurus from Wyoming, Utah, and Colorado during the Upper Jurassic. The Bronosaurus loves to roam around the flood plains and lakes munching on anything green from grass to leafy plants. Similarly the Brontoprumpus likes to gather up lots of green cash as well as play on the leafy greens, as he rides around in a golf cart at one of his clubs. Plus he likes munching on the media and anyone who gets in his way, and he has attracted a big following who have given him plenty of greenbacks for his campaigns to keep the presidency or to win it back after he loses.

The Brontotrumpus

The Stegotrumpus is very much like the 30 ton 20 foot Stegosaurus, a plant-eater from Wyoming, Utah, and Colorado during the Upper Jurassic. The Stegosaurus is always ready to defend itself at the slightest opportunity, and it uses its big tail to slap and whap anyone who dares attack. Should anyone come after it, it is eager to strike back with all it's got, using everything from threats to charging again and again, until any would-be predators slink away, afraid to make the Stegosaurus madder and more deadly.

Likewise, the Stegotrumpus is ever ready to attack, whether by angry tweets to fire someone, calling someone an insulting name, or filing mostly failing lawsuits with claims of fraud. It figures if it just slaps and whaps enough, anyone who tries to fight back will give up and go away. But while some do, many are now fighting back, claiming the law and constitution are on their side.

The Stegotrumpus

The Trumpatops is very much like the 30 foot 6 ton Triceratops, from the flood plains and swamp forests of Wyoming, Montana, and Alberta during the Upper Cretaceous. The Triceratops is ever ready to go on a rampage. If anyone poses a threat, he's aggressive in protecting his herd of followers, and he is willing, ready, and able to confront just about anyone about anything. Similarly, the Trumpatops is scrappy and pugnacious, unwilling to take anything from anyone, while he gives out whatever he wants, and he supports the team around him when they strike out at anyone who comes too close.

Also, the Triceratops uses its deadly horns to fight fiercly, like a wound-up trap ready to spring once anything startles it, so others beware its fury, or else. Likewise, the Trumpatops is ready to take offense at the hint of anyone daring to not agree with anything he says, and he expects his staffers and supporters to parrot any claims, even if they are easily provable lies -- over 20,000 of them in the last four years. And the Trumpatops keeps adding more and more lies, using them like an ever-growing shield around himself to keep out the truth.

The Trumpatops

The Spinotrumpus is very much like the 30 foot 3 ton Spinosaurus, a meat-eating scavenger from the floodplains of Egypt during the Upper Cretaceous. Just like the Spinosaurus might spin around while looking for dead carcasses to scavenge, so the Spinotrumpis often puts a spin on things to appear in the best light. Then, if challenged, he can easily spin things around to make what's false appear true or claim what's true is false. And that can leave those who are listening or reporting the news spinning.

Also, the Spinotrumpis can often play nice and later spin around and launch an attack when least expected. Or if a competitor or the media tries to spin anything, he can spin away and rebound with another attack that can put anyone in a tailspin, so they're spinning and spinning, until they either go along with his spin or crash and burn. Then, the Spinotrumpus can spin on to find the next victim to attack.

Spinotrumpus

The Iguanoramus Trump is much like the 30 foot 6 ton plant-eating Iguanodon, who frequented the swamps and lakes of England and Belgium during the Lower Cretaceous. The Iguanodon was known for fighting fierce and dirty to fight off rivals and defend against predators with the large menacing spikes on his front feet. And just like the Iguanodon, the Inguanaoramus Trump fights fierce and dirty.

But maybe more accurately, he might be called a Trumpus ignoramus, because he doesn't know what he doesn't know, doesn't care that he doesn't know it, or doesn't admit that he knows it, as least publically, because the facts don't fit his latest theory. He would rather deny the facts, such as about climate change and the pandemic, so he can claim they don't exist or go away. This way, he can avoid acknowledging that the planet and people are dying due to the warming climate and the spreading virus. No wonder he's such an iguanoramus -- uh, ignoramus.

Iguanoramos Trumpus

The Hadrotrumpus is very much like the Hadrosauraus, a 30 foot, 3-4 ton plant eater from the New Jersey swamps during the Late Cretaceous). The Hadrosauraus can run fast on his hind legs when necessary, though he mostly runs on all fours. It all depends on whether he's running away or running to something.

Similarly, the Hadrotrumpus is doing a lot of running these days -- from running from debts and civil suits against him and his companies to running from possible criminal charges now that he seems to have finally run out of runs. Still, it's hard to know where he is running, since he's constantly changing course. But just as the Hadrosaurus has plenty of bite with his mouthful of teeth to grind up the competition, so the Hadrotrumpus is ready to put the bite on anyone to get money or to take down his rivals.

Hadrotrumpus

FLYING AND MARINE REPTILES

The Trumpdactyl is much like the flying Pterodactyl with a 3 foot wingspan that flew around North America, Europe, Australia, and Africa from the Jurassic to Cretaceous periods. The Peterodactyl flew around seeking small insects and animals as its prey, and when it saw a likely victim, it swooped down for the kill.

Likewise, the Trumodactyl is ready to swoop in on its victims. Then, he takes advantage of them or destroys them in various ways -- such as by not paying contractors, suing critics for defamation, delaying court trials so plaintiffs run out of time or money, and calling anyone opposing him insulting, demeaning names on Twitter or at his rallies.

The Trumpodactyl

The Quezalotrumpus is also much like the 150 pound Quetzalcoatlus, the largest flying reptile with a 40 foot wingspan. The Quetzalcoatlus loved to feed on fish and scavenge dead kill throughout Texas during the Upper Cretaceous, and it was one of the most fearsome reptile of those times.

Likewise, the Quezalorumpus has flown all over in the Air-Force One jet, and he has found a growing number of victims everywhere. These include Allies he has abandoned by pulling out of mutual support agreements like NATO or pulling aid away from allies like the Kurds. Then, too, he supported an air strike again a top Iranian general Qassim Soleimani. Additionally, like the super scavenger Quetzalcoatlus, the Quezalotrumpus was eager to make a killing in other huge deals -- from building a hotel to creating another golf course, where he can easily find more business deals from the guests.

Quetzalotrumpus

The Mosatrumpus is much like the 56 foot 15 ton Mosasaurus, who was the terror of the shallow seas throughout Europe and North America in the Late Cretaceous. He ate fish and other marine animals and was a fierce and fast predator.

Likewise, the Mostrumpus is a fearsome terror who seeks to conquer others and rule by fear so he gets his way. That's how he gradually exerted his power to take over the Republican party by cowing anyone who disagreed with him out of fear. As a result, during his Presidency, very few were willing to publically stand up to him though many complained to each other and sometimes the press about Trump's latest wrong actions, scandals, or lies. But now it seems he over-estimated his power, since he was voted out of office and his attempts to use lawsuits or appeals to change the election failed. So now his ability to terrorize and conquer others has waned.

The Mosatrumpus

BIRDS

The Dodo Trump might be compared to the 3 foot tall 25 to 47 pounds Dodo Bird, who wandered around the Island of Mauritius from the beginning of the Paleocene to the mid-17th century. There the Dodo Bird fed on nuts, seeds, bulbs, roots, and fruits, but he found it hard going when he faced new predators, as climate change and deforestation destroyed his island retreat, leading to his extinction.

Similarly, the Dodo Trump has been up against climate change, which has led to more frequent and intense tropical storms and to a growing wildfire menace in California and other states. Even so, just like the Dodo Bird became extinct in part due to climate change, the Dodo Trump has repeatedly denied that the climate is changing. So that's one reason he is often considered a big dodo, and many new opponents are gathering, from Democrats to the media and even Fox News, so he won't be able to retreat much more.

The Dodo Trump

The Great Trump Terror Bird is also much like the 7 foot tall, 330 pound flightless Giant Terror Bird, also known as the Titanis, named after the titans, who were ancient Greek gods. As a meat-eater and scavenger, the Giant Terror Bird roamed the open savanna of Florida during the Pliocene to early Pleistocene and was the largest predatory bird that ever lived. He used his huge beak like an ax to kill his prey.

In like fashion, the Great Trump Terror Bird has used his big mouth to kill an adversary with insulting and humiliating words. So anyone working or dealing with the Giant Trump Terror Bird has had to be careful, or he would pounce and destroy, using insulting words like weapons to upset or ruin the reputation of an opponent, from Hillary Clinton to Dr. Anthony Fauci. But now more and more opponents have gathered to shoot down the Trump Terror Bird with their votes, undermine his lawsuits, or otherwise get him out of offices, so he will cease terrorizing everyone he confronts.

Giant Trump Terror Bird

MAMMALS

The Woolly Rhinotrump is much like the 12 foot 2 ton Woolly Rhino, who roamed around the Americas eating plants from the Pliocene to the end of the Pleistocene. The Wholly Rhino is known for his short temper, like most rhinos. So if he felt challenged or confronted by anything, he was quick to fume and snort in anger, so his challenger or opponent would quickly back down and go away.

Likewise, the Wholly Rhinotrump is easily angered and has raged all around the White House and has tweeted out angry blasts on Twitter. But when challengers stand firm, sometimes he has backed down, such as agreeing to an initial economic stimulus for the unemployed or deciding not to pull all the troops out of Afghanistan and Iraq, because military leaders said that would be unsafe. But in other cases, he has angrily pressed ahead and has done what he wants to get publicity or money, such as when he staged a photo shoot in front of a church near the White House and invited the military to tear gas any protestors in the way to get them to leave.

Woolly Rhinotrump

The Woolly Trumpoth shares many characteristics with the 9 foot 2-3 ton Woolly Mammoth, a plant-eater who traveled in herds like modern elephants through Asia, Europe, Alaska, and Canada during the Pleistocene. Just like the Woolly Mammoth sought to gather as large a herd as possible and was ready to trample anyone not in his herd, the Woolly Trumpoth has been ready to push out anyone who was not a loyal follower.

Likewise, just like the Woolly Mammoth roared loudly, tossed around his heavy trunk to scare off anyone threatening to take prey from his herd, and stood ready to squash prey with his big foot, the Woolly Trumpoth makes a lot of noise and has tossed around insults, lawsuits, and other threats to defeat any challengers or anyone offending him.

Then, too, much like the Woolly Mammoth was always easy to find, because he left large footprints in his wake, the Woolly Trumpoth has done the same. That's because he has had a large entourage of secret service protectors, family members, lawyers, senior advisers, and staffers all around him and ready to do his bidding at his beck and call. And if things don't go his way, he has been ready to roar even louder through a deluge of tweets on Twitter, often with words, sentences, or the whole tweet in CAPS, which is like roaring for emphasis and attention today.

The Woolly Trumpoth

The Giant Trump Sloth shares many characteristics with the 20 foot 4 ton Giant Ground Sloth or Megatherium, who ate plants throughout the Americas during the Pliocene to the end of the Pleistocene. The Giant Ground Sloth is known for sometimes being slow moving and not overly bright.

Similarly, the Giant Trump Sloth hasn't always stayed up with the times and has been especially dimwitted in knowing about anything outside of his usual stomping grounds. It's just foreign to him, so he hasn't thought he has to know about it, such as not reading intelligence briefings and playing golf instead of attending a coronavirus meeting with G20 leaders.

Another similarity is that a Giant Ground Sloth who responds too quickly could easily fall into a trap. Then, he could be truly dangerous when cornered, since he could quickly strike back with the three huge claws on each front foot. Likewise, the Giant Trump Sloth has been especially vengeful in fighting back against losing the election and conceding to Joe Biden, such as by filing lawsuit after lawsuit to overturn the results in key states. Then, when that didn't work, he tried reaching out to state officials to invalidate the state results to keep him in office. Plus he waited for about three weeks to prevent a transition from going forward, despite the growing danger to national security.

Giant Trump Sloth

EARLY APES AND HUMANS

The Gigantotrumpus shares characteristics with the 9 foot tall, 1200 pound Gigantopithicus, who used to roam the bamboo forests of China, Vietnam, and Indonesia munching on bamboo, fruit and seeds during the Pleistocene. The Gigantopitihicus is known as the largest ape or primate to exist and is possibly the source of the Yeti and Bigfoot legends and sightings.

Likewise, the Gigantotrumpus sought to be as big as possible, and for the past four years, kept increasing the powers of the President with executive orders. But for the last few months the Gigantotrumps has been mainly been sighted playing golf and tweeting out complaints about his election loss, along with appeals to his supporters for more and more money. And now, perhaps he may become a source of legends and rare sightings as he retreats from the White House, perhaps to Mar-A-Logo in Florida.

Gigantotrumpus

The Homo Trumpilis might be compared to the 3 to 4.5 foot 70 pound Homo Habilis, who lived in Africa 2.8 to 1.5 million years ago during the Pleistocene. The Homo Habilis was the first stone tool maker and user, and is known as an ape-like human who has mastered all kinds of tools.

Today, the Homo Trumpilis has mastered all kinds of White House tools, such as using Executive Orders, firing staffers and agency heads considered disloyal, and hiring loyalists to carry out his orders. He also loves tooling around in all kinds of ways – from riding in luxury cars and vans to super-fast sleek planes.

While the Homo Habilis has been called the "Handy Man" because of his use of hand tools, now the Homo Trumpilis might be called the "Trump Man," because of the way Trump has tried to trump everyone with his yells and calls to bring in the military to confront protestors. But now it seems he got out trumped by the Democrats and Joe Biden.

Homo Trumpilis

The Trumpo Erectus shares some characteristics with the 4-6 foot 90-150 pound Homo Erectus, who roamed through Africa, the Mediterranean, and Western Asia from 1.9 million to 70,000 years ago during the Pleistocene. The Homo Erectus was the first to use language, control fire, and migrate out of Africa.

Unfortunately, the Trump Erectus' use of language has remained very coarse, and he is especially known for his grunts, yells, and short phrases, such as "That's huge!" and "You're a loser!" However, his ability to control fire has certainly evolved, as he has eagerly fired anyone and everyone who has dared to oppose or contradict him. He has also developed an ability to get his fervent supporters fired up, so they are ready to attack his latest foe, such as with death threats, hate-filled graffiti, and even assassination attempts. He has also continue to migrate everywhere, as he has found places to put hotels, golf courses, and casinos all over the globe, though not all have stayed there, as a result of his failing profits and bankruptcies that have taken them down.

Trumpo Erectus

The Neandertrump also is like the Neanderthal, a 5 foot tall, 140 pound early human who lived and hunted throughout Africa and Eurasia 400,000 to 28,000 years ago in the Late Pleistocene. The Neanderthals made advanced stone tools, ornamental objects, and jewelry, built shelters, wore clothing from animal pelts, had a language, buried their dead, and lived in complex family groups. They also struggled to survive in a hostile environment.

Today, the Neandertrump has been doing much the same, though he spends much more and makes everything much bigger than before, such as in buying expensive jewelry, suits, and gowns from pricey stores, and traveling in luxury cars and private planes from place to place. He has a very complex family group, too, with three wives and dozens of children and grandchildren from different wives. Plus, like his ancestors, he has continued the tradition of keeping woman in their place to show them who's boss. He also loves to show off all his trophies, from his hotels and branded items to his current trophy wife. Even acquiring the White House for four years might be considered one more trophy, and he hated to give it up in the end.

Neandertrump

The Homo Trumpus Trumpus is a newly developed subspecies of modern humans, who is especially known for his big head which contains his big ego. He commonly uses his short-stubby fingers to point out opponents who need to be silenced and removed from his presence. He is especially known for his ability to entertain, such as when he makes stupid and silly statements or plays dumb when asked questions he can't answer, such as about foreign policy. Additionally, he is known for his ability to be cunning and wily, like a fox, so he readily evades or hides from any question or person he doesn't like. And like a snake, scorpion, or other predator, he can quickly bite, sting, poison, or otherwise attack and seek to destroy those who oppose him - from calling them suckers and losers to firing them if they are on his staff or in an agency he controls. If criticized for any actions, nothing is ever his fault – it is always someone else who did something wrong. Then, he goes on to give the next rousing speech or tweet to his supporters, who are ready to rush to his aid and attack his foes -- from mounting protests to beating up opponents to planning attacks on government officials, like the governor of Michigan.

Homo Trumpus Trumpus

The Homo Trumpien is another new subspecies of Homo Sapiens, who is known for his very aggressive, destructive nature. Sometimes called names by his opponents, like "narcissist," "sociopath," and "egomaniac," he easily ignores any insults or criticisms by claiming the opponent is dead wrong, while wishing he or she was simply dead. Unfortunately he often has grandiose grand plans which don't work out, such as building a wall that never got finished. Or he bullies others into supporting his plans that fail, such as getting the Senate Republicans to support his attempts to undo the election results. So he is constantly overcoming one misfortune or dangerous escapade after another.

Still he continues to rise like the phoenix, only to be shot down again after another perilous flight that destroys others who come along for the ride. Even so, he is sure his next project will be "really great," "very huge," the "best of the best." But even as he builds more and more, he destroys more and more. And many of his actions have helped to undermine the American economy, such as his efforts to ignore the pandemic for months, thinking it would go away; his trade wars with China's and other countries; and his repeated denials of climate change. And his great extravagances and excesses, combined with his frequent braggadocio, have earned him the title of the biggest liar, too.

Homo Trumpien

THE EVOLUTION OF HUMANS AND HOPE FOR THE FUTURE

In sum, Trump is like many animals and early humans who have gone extinct. And now Trump lost the election given the qualities he shared with many animals and early humans who went extinct, such as those reflected in the following illustration showing the evolution of humans.

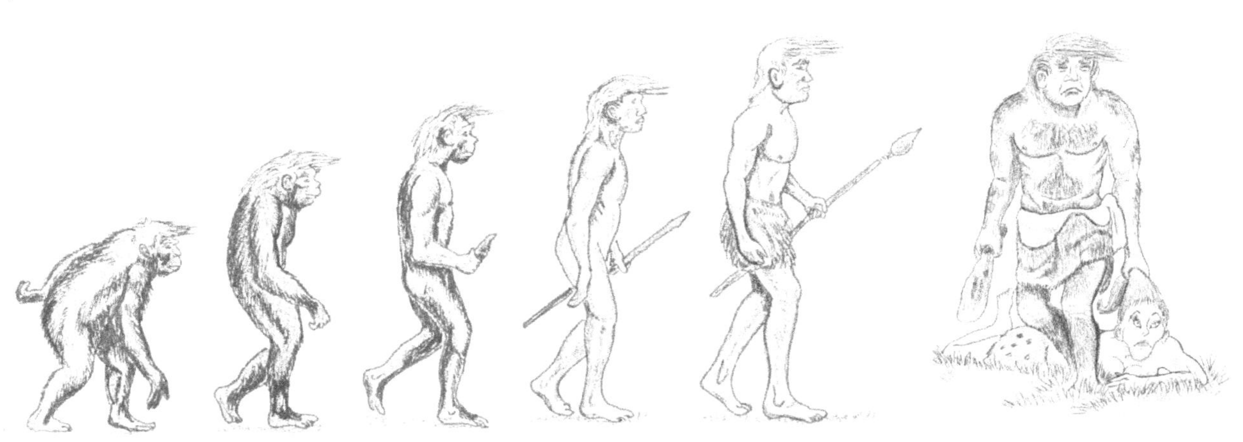

Evolution to the Neandertrump

THE EVOLUTION OF HUMANS

New – Revised Based on the Latest News

Old – Based on Past Scientific Evidence

But now there is hope for the future now that Trump lost and there is a new Biden-Harris administration. So let us hope.

ABOUT THE AUTHOR

Sandi Derring - Author

Sandi Derring is an author who has long been following the ups and downs of Trump's 2016 campaign, White House years, 2020 election, and final defeat. She also supports science, preserving the environment, recognizing climate control, and eradicating the coronavirus -- all things Trump is against or has chosen to ignore.

She has been inspired to write this book in the spirit of hope for the future now that Trump has lost the election, but just in case, she is using a pseudonym, like the illustrator. After all there are about 73 million voters who voted for Trump, and you never know, some of them could be dangerous lunatics, unless they understand why Trump and Trumpism lost at the polls.

ABOUT THE ILLUSTRATOR

Nick Alexander - Illustrator

Writer/artist Nick Alexander was born and raised in New Jersey in a boating family. His first short story was published at the age of 14 in a national magazine. He has since written stage and screenplays some of which have won awards and been produced and numerous short stories. His traditionally published novels include historical fiction, fantasy. and science fiction. His illustrations have appeared in various publications from children's picture books to political cartoons in newspapers and online. He presently resides outside Sedona, Arizona.

THE A-Z LIST
Los Angeles, California
bookpub@att.net